This Orchard
book belongs to

For the lovely ladies Liz and Giselle,
without whom this book wouldn't exist!

ORCHARD BOOKS

First published in Great Britain in 2008 by Orchard Books
This edition published in 2020 by The Watts Publishing Group

1 3 5 7 9 10 8 6 4 2

Text and illustrations © Sam Lloyd, 2008

The moral rights of the author-illustrator have been asserted.

A CIP catalogue record for this book is available from the British Library.

ISBN 978 1 40836 075 0

Printed and bound in China

MIX
Paper from
responsible sources
FSC
www.fsc.org   FSC® C104740

Orchard Books
An imprint of Hachette Children's Group
Part of The Watts Publishing Group Limited
Carmelite House
50 Victoria Embankment
London EC4Y 0DZ

An Hachette UK Company
www.hachette.co.uk

www.hachettechildrens.co.uk

Mr Pusskins

BEST IN SHOW

Sam Lloyd

BEST-
LOOKING
PET

ORCHARD

This is the story of a little girl called Emily, and her dear cat, Mr Pusskins.

One morning, while flicking through the paper, Emily spotted something — there was a pet show in town that very day!

PET SHOW
COMES TO TOWN

Bring along your beloved pet to be judged by our panel of top experts. Please bear in mind that standards will be very high and only the finest of pets may enter. Contestants must be one year and over.

"Oh, Mr Pusskins! You're such a handsome boy, you simply must enter!" gushed Emily.

But Mr Pusskins wasn't so keen . . .

Little Whiskers, Emily's dear kitten,
was too young to enter the competition.
"We can both support Mr Pusskins instead,"
said Emily, excitedly.
Mr Pusskins glared at the other contestants.
Why did they look so snazzy for such
a silly show?

But as soon as Mr Pusskins entered the
arena, he knew it was because of . . .

...the
TROPHY!

It was the most fabulous thing Mr Pusskins had ever seen. He simply **had** to have it!

He hurried to the dressing room, where . . .

he licked . . . .

and slicked . . .

and buffed and fluffed . . .

. . . until he was **magnificent!**

When Mr Pusskins joined the other pets they gasped in amazement. Surely he'd win and the trophy would be his!

Just then, they heard an announcement . . .

Mr Pusskins wondered where the judging would take place – luckily Madame Fifi seemed keen to show him where to go.

Mr Pusskins raced off. There was not a moment to lose. He must win the competition and get his paws on that trophy! Madame Fifi trotted away in the other direction.

But hang on, this wasn't where he should be! Drat! That dirty, double~crossing poodle must have tricked him!

Mr Pusskins had to get to the judging – fast!
He needed to take a short cut.

Mr Pusskins
leapt over
a fence . . .

zoomed into
a tunnel . . .

zipped between
some flags . . .

pounced through
a hoop . . .

. . . and arrived at the judging, just in time.
He hoped no one would notice his mishap!

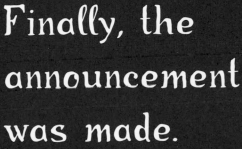

Mr Pusskins waited anxiously. He wanted that trophy so much.

Finally, the announcement was made.

"And the winner is ..."

". . . MADAME FIFI FOU-FOU!"
MONSIEUR DE LA STICK
TROUBADOUR THE TRIUMPHANT
BUNNYK THE BEAUTIFUL
BEST-LOOKING PET
MR PUSSKINS
MADAME FIFI FOU-FOU

Mr Pusskins was **mortified**.
He couldn't bear to watch his precious
trophy go to that **cheating** dog.
He had to find Emily and tell her everything.

Emily squeezed Mr Pusskins tight.
"There, there, darling. Never you mind," she soothed. "We both know Madame Fifi didn't deserve to win."
Suddenly, there was another announcement!

"Mr Pusskins
has won the Top Talent Trophy!"

"Mr Pusskins! The way you zipped through
the obstacle course was incredible!"
exclaimed the judge. "Please accept
our most spectacular Top Talent Trophy!"
Mr Pusskins purred with pleasure.

This is the end of the story of a little girl called Emily, and her dear cat, Mr Pusskins. Even though the trophy is in pride of place . . .

Emily doesn't need it to prove how wonderful
Mr Pusskins is . . .

because she's always known!